KiNG
FLASHYPANTS
AND THE BOO-HOO WITCHES

HODDER CHILDREN'S BOOKS

First published in Great Britain in 2018 by Hodder and Stoughton

3 5 7 9 10 8 6 4 2

A CIP catalogue record for this book is available from the British Library.

ISBN 978 1 444 94097 8

Edited by Emma Goldhawk

Printed and bound in Great Britain by CPI Group (UK) Ltd,
Croydon, CR0 4YY.

The paper and board used in this book are from well-managed forests and
other responsible sources.

Hodder Children's Books
An imprint of Hachette Children's Group
Part of Hodder & Stoughton
Carmelite House, 50 Victoria Embankment
London EC4Y 0DZ

An Hachette UK Company
www.hachette.co.uk

www.hachettechildrens.co.uk

KING FLASHYPANTS

AND THE BOO-HOO
THE WITCHES

h

*Hodder
Children's
Books*

WRITTEN AND DRAWN BY ANDY RILEY

With thanks to Polly Faber,
Emma Goldhawk, Samuel Perrett,
Anne McNeil, Gordon Wise,
Niall Harman, Hilary Murray Hill,
Emily Thomas and Kevin Cecil

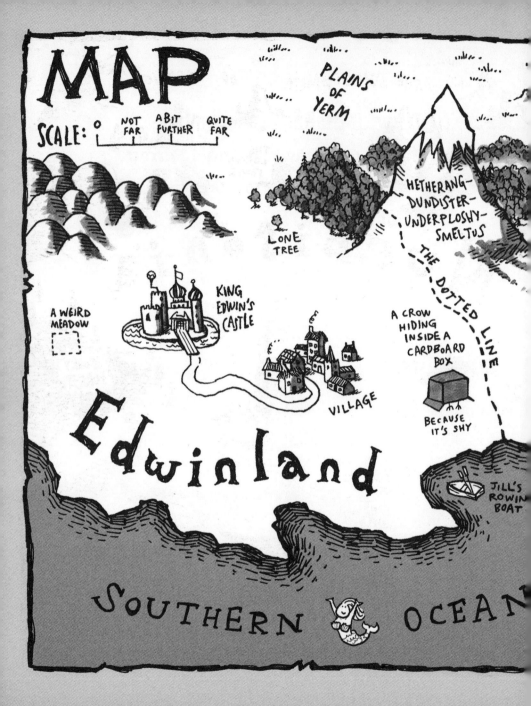

Twelve Chapters to Blow Your Mind

Wheeeeeeeee

A nine-year-old boy sat at the top of a slide.
He wasn't an ordinary boy. He was King Edwin
Flashypants. You could tell he was a king
because he had a gleaming crown and an 'I am
a king' certificate on his bedroom wall.

And because this boy was a king, with his

own castle and suit of armour and a catapult
which could fire jam sandwiches into his mouth,
he wasn't sat on an ordinary slide. No no-ne-no.

It was a slide he'd just finished building – the only one in the world with two loop-the-loops in it. And King Edwin was about to be the first slider ever to slide down this slide.

GENTLY DOES IT, YOUR MAJESTY,

said Minister Jill, the grown-up who helped Edwin with the hard parts of being a king.

"It's perfectly safe, Jill!" said Edwin. "I know my last slide fell to bits, but this time but I've held it together with different string."

"Thicker string?"

"No, a nicer colour."

"Then I'm sure it'll be fine," said Jill, clenching her teeth, holding her breath and shutting her eyes.

"I'll get a picture of your epic sliding, Your Majesty!" said Megan the Jester. She was Edwin's best friend. She would have taken a photograph, but this was the olden days, and they hadn't invented cameras. She'd just have to draw really fast.

In the olden days, loads of things we know

hadn't been invented yet. There were no buses,

so everyone had to ride around on small angry

goats. If you wanted to watch a
funny video of a kitten falling off
a sofa, you had to sit and wait a
thousand years for
someone to make the
first computer. And it's
hard to sit and wait for
a thousand years because
sooner or later you'll need to
go for a wee.

Edwin pushed himself
down the slide.
Zoom! He went
round the first loop.

Zoom! Around the second loop.

Faster and faster.

Then – **WHOOSH!** – he shot off the end of the slide and went sailing through the air.

This is great! Edwin thought. *And perfectly safe, because I'll land on that big pile of velvet cushions we fetched from my throne room.*

But Edwin was travelling much too fast. He shot straight over the cushions.

Whoops! thought the king. *So much for the cushions. I hope I don't land on anything too sharp.*

Edwinland wasn't big, so there was only one village in it, and that was called Village. And because that day was the 35th of Apritember, the villagers were holding their monthly Market of Sharp Things. Dozens of stalls, all crammed with the most jagged and spiky stuff money could buy.

Edwin looked down and saw the 'Brambles and Open Scissors' stall.

Hope I don't land on that, he thought.

He zoomed straight over it.

Next was the 'Badger Teeth and Table Corners' stall.

Really really hope I don't land on that, thought King Edwin.

And he flew straight over it. But he was dropping quickly now. So it was lucky for Edwin that the market's food stall only sold marshmallows, and they had just made the world's biggest.

WOooMMMpp!

Edwin vanished into the big pink sugary blob. It took him fifteen minutes to eat his way out.

"Here's the picture, Your Majesty!" said Megan. Edwin had been flying so fast through the air that Megan only managed to draw his hand and some of his bum.

"I love it!" said Edwin. "And now – well, actually, once we've moved the velvet cushions along a bit – I'm giving this slide to all the children of Edwinland! Get sliding, everyone!"

Edwin was a good king who loved to share his best things.

Everybody had a terrific afternoon sliding and flying and splatting into velvet cushions, while Jill bustled about saying grown-up things like 'mind how you go' and 'try not to lose a leg'.

Then it was teatime. Back home at the castle, the king and the jester noshed on big slices of gold on toast. But Edwin wasn't totally happy. It took him a moment to work out why.

"Megan, I'm not totally happy and I've worked out why," said Edwin. "Now I've built a two-loop slide, I can't think of what we should do next. This kingdom isn't so big. Have we been everywhere and done everything?"

They really had done a lot of things. They'd
gone water-skiing in the moat. They'd taken it
in turns to go in the stocks and get custard pies
in the face.

"We've never explored The Weird Meadow,"
said Megan.

The Weird Meadow was a place in Edwinland where nobody went, because Minister Jill asked them all not to.

Jill had a lot of rules. 'Don't eat your ear wax when other kings and queens come for dinner' – that was one. 'After you've used a battle-axe, put it away' – that was another.

"I'll ask her nicely," said Edwin, and he went to find Minister Jill, who was counting out piles of silver coins to pay for the giant marshmallow.

Jill had to work hard, even when everyone else was playing.

Some days she wondered if anyone would ever notice just how hard.

"Jill? Minister Jill? Jill?" said the king. "Please please please please please please can me and Megan—"

"Your Majesty," said Jill. "I was about to come and find you because we might need a new rule. 'Let's try not to land in giant marshmallows because they cost a teensy bit more than we think.' But sorry, what were you asking me?"

Edwin did his grumpy-chops face. *She*

stopped me talking AND just gave me another

rule, thought Edwin. *Why can't she be fun like*

Megan?

Edwin was a bit annoyed – and when he was like that, he sometimes said things he wasn't proud of later.

"Edwinland is supposed to be a fun kingdom, Jill!" said Edwin. "If you don't like that, I just don't know why you're here."

Jill was quiet for a bit. Then Edwin stomped away to find Megan.

"When you go to bed tonight, Megan, try not to fall asleep," said Edwin.

Then he leaned very close and said:

"We're going exploring."

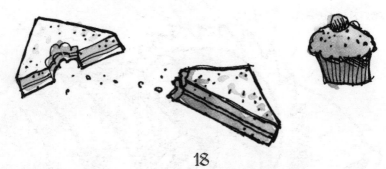

The Weird Meadow

When Edwin and Megan left the castle, it was
so late at night that really it was very early the
next morning. The sun wasn't up yet. It was still
behind the hills, yawning and pulling the duvet
over its head.

"We're breaking a whole load of Minister Jill's rules, so let's be super-quiet to be sure we don't wake her up," shouted Megan. She would have whispered it, but she needed to make sure Edwin heard.

They both climbed on their small angry
goats and rode them through the dark lanes of
Edwinland. Small angry goats went very fast,
and once they started they never liked to stop,
so the only way to get off a small angry goat

was to dive into a hedge.

Edwin and Megan climbed out of the hedge, and there it was in front of them: The Weird Meadow. But it was completely surrounded by a stone wall twice as tall as Megan. Luckily there was a huge sign nearby which said PLEASE DO NOT ENTER THE WEIRD MEADOW.

When they leaned the sign against the wall, it made a very handy ramp.

Edwin thought: *We're being quite naughty. And Jill would only say* don't go to The Weird Meadow *for a good reason. I sort of want to turn back, but I'm too embarrassed to say so.*

It's not just children who think this kind of thought. So do adults, sometimes about really important things. That's just one of the ways that adults aren't quite as clever as they make out.

King Edwin and Megan scrambled down the far side of the wall, only grazing three out of their four knees, and had a good look round. It was a perfectly normal looking field, about the size of a football pitch.

Just grass and a few weeds," said Edwin.

"Nothing very weird about this meadow at
all," said Megan the Jester.

"The buttercup just spoke," Edwin whispered to Megan.

"I know. It's freaking my loaf," said Megan. "That's a new cool way of saying, 'I'm amazed.' I just thought it up."

"I like it," said Edwin.

BAM! Edwin was knocked off his feet by a tortoise going faster than a galloping horse.

"GROWL!" said a tiger, as it jumped onto Megan's nose. The tiger was the size of a beetle.

"Excuse me," said a train-sized millipede as it rumbled between them.

"Do you know what I think, Megan?" said Edwin. "I think this meadow is a bit weird after all."

"It's a big sack of strange and no mistake," said Megan.

Right in the middle of the field, next to a pile of rocks, was a sign which said 'Do Not Move These Rocks'.

"Let's move these rocks!" said Edwin.

Under the rocks they found a metal box. Painted on it were the words:

DON'T OPEN THIS METAL BOX

"Let's open this metal box!" said Edwin.

"Gosh, Your Majesty," said Megan, "You really don't like doing what the signs say, do you?"

No, I don't, thought Edwin. *Turns out being naughty is a bit of a thrill, like when you use all the bubble bath in one go.*

Edwin hoped the box might have pirate treasure in it, or something really fun like a load of human skulls. But all they found inside was a wooden stick. He was about to throw it away when he saw a paper tag on it, which said:

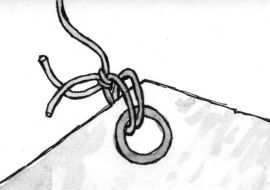

OKAY, YOU'VE IGNORED ALL THE OTHER MESSAGES BUT **PLEASE** DON'T IGNORE THIS ONE. WHAT YOU HAVE IN YOUR HAND IS A MAGIC WAND. *A VERY POWERFUL WAND.* EVERY LITTLE BIT OF IT IS CRAMMED WITH A TON OF MAGIC, SO MUCH THAT THE MAGIC LEAKS OUT, AND THAT'S WHAT MAKES THE WEIRD MEADOW SO WEIRD.

THE WAND REMEMBERS ALL THE SPELLS IT'S EVER CAST. AND MOST SPELLS RHYME. SO WHATEVER HAPPENS, DON'T MAKE A RHYME NEAR THIS WAND. YOU ARE NOT QUALIFIED TO DO MAGIC STUFF.

I REPEAT:

DO NOT RHYME.

That looks like Jill's writing, thought Edwin. *But it can't be – we're in The Weird Meadow, so she could only put the note here if she broke one of her own rules. Jill would never do that!*

"Let's be careful here, Megan," said Edwin. "I'd hate to be a stupid king, so now I'm putting down this ... object."

That was close, thought Edwin. *I nearly said 'thing' and made a rhyme by mistake.*

"Good idea," said Megan, "A magic wand might be dangerous. Hey! Imagine if it shot out lightning. Wouldn't that be awfully—"

Edwin ran to Megan to cover her mouth before she said the word he thought she was about to say. And he would have made it too, if

the speedy tortoise hadn't tripped him over again.

"... frightening," said Megan.

With a

KRAKK–KOOM!

and a

WOZZZEEE!

and a

GRA–POWW!,

the wand leapt from the box. It bounced all

over the place, shooting searing bolts of

lightning in all directions. This was magic

lightning, so it came in all colours – yellow, orange, purple, and an olden-days colour you don't see any more called clowngrumble.

It lit up the clouds for miles around. It zapped the tortoise, fizzed the millipede and tickled the tiger.

"I'll get it! I'll get it!" said Megan. She dodged three lightning bolts, grabbed the magic wand in mid-air, threw it back into the metal box and slammed the lid.

"Whoops," said Megan. "Sorry about that."

"We should leave that thing right here." said King Edwin, "It's not safe."

"Totally," said Megan the Jester.

"But if we did take the wand home, because it's sort of amazing and cool, if we took it, we wouldn't need to tell Jill, would we?" said Edwin.

They carried the metal box with the wand inside back to the castle. It was a quiet night. So quiet that Edwin could hear sounds from far away.

The wind blew in from the southern seas - and on that wind, a voice singing a sad song. Edwin couldn't quite hear the words.

Something something something something
***Can't find** something something.*
*Something **up** something something.*
Something something something.

That's how it went. But who was singing?
Why were they so sad?

Another mystery.

Edwin loved mysteries. He sometimes
wondered what happened to farts after you've
smelt them. They just seemed to vanish. But
where do they go?

I'll find it all out one day, thought the king.

The Thing About Jill

A few hours later, Edwin, Megan and Jill ate breakfast in the throne room. Nobody spoke. There was just the chippity-chip of Jill taking the top off her boiled egg.

Jill looks like she's getting ready to say something, thought King Edwin. *I wonder what? I'm pretty sure I haven't said anything to make her upset.*

Edwin wasn't always good at remembering what he'd said the day before.

Jill was stirring her coffee for just a bit too long. Tinkly-tink tink-tink. Tink.

Wow, she really is getting ready to say something, thought Edwin. *I wonder if she's about to call me 'Your Majesty'? Sometimes that means she's a bit unhappy.*

"Your Majesty," said Jill. "Yesterday you said you didn't know why I was in Edwinland, but sometimes I don't know if you notice everything that goes on in this castle. Like breakfast. Breakfast doesn't just happen, you know."

"Doesn't it?" said Edwin.

"No, somebody has to lay the table, and buy the baguettes and the cornflakes, and guess who that is?"

Edwin had never really thought about it much.

"Well," said Jill, "the nice person who sorted all that out might just be sitting in front of ..."

Minister Jill stopped, and looked over Edwin's shoulder.

"That's odd," said Jill, "why are there muddy footprints on the floor? At breakfast time?"

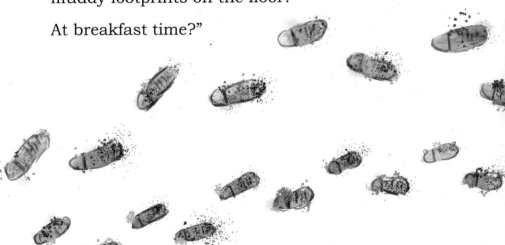

"Don't know!" said Edwin. "We haven't been outside in the night, have we, Megan? It's all completely normal. It's just a totally normal breakfast, and everything's normal."

"And we both came straight from our beds, where we've definitely been sleeping all night," said Megan.

Jill looked at Edwin, then at Megan. She kept looking at Megan for a long time.

Then she put down her knife and fork.

"Megan. Edwin. Is there anything you need to tell me?" Jill said.

"Well, I've got a sore thumb today," said Megan. "It's a bit red and swollen. Don't know why."

"I saw that," said Jill. " I also saw that twenty seconds ago you grew a pair of antlers, Megan."

Megan felt around her face. She was pretty sure she didn't used to have giant stag horns coming out of the side of her head. But she definitely did now.

"We kind of ... the thing is ..." said Edwin. "Oh, Minister Jill, we went to The Weird Meadow. I'm sorry."

"And you found something there, didn't you?" said Jill. "Show me, please."

Edwin went behind his throne, pulled out the metal box and opened it for Jill.

"Turns out that thing's not just a twig. It's a magic wand," said Megan.

"Oh, I know just what it is," said Jill. "It's time I told you two a story. A story about a young girl."

"Hey," Megan whispered in Edwin's ear. "I hope this is one of the stories with a twist at the end where she says 'and that young girl was me!'"

"Oi, Megan, no spoilers," said Edwin.

And Jill began her story.

"Once there was a young girl, and this young girl's mother was a witch. The very worst kind of witch. A Boo-Hoo Witch.

"There were three Boo-Hoo Witches, and they lived far away across the ocean on the Island of the Weeping Willow. Boo-Hoo Witches love to cast spells which spoil people's lives and make them cry. And every time they make someone cry, the Boo-Hoo Witches become more powerful.

"One day, that girl's mother died. So the two witches wanted the girl to take her mother's place. They taught her wicked spells – how to make people cry by turning their teddy bears into giant wasps, or their birthday cakes into zombie heads. But the girl wasn't like her mum! The girl didn't like things to be all twisted and wrong! She wanted to be helpful and kind, and she wouldn't make anyone cry if she could help it.

"So, on her twelfth birthday, when those two nasty witches were about to make her a full

Boo-Hoo Witch, with a witch watch
and everything, that girl grabbed her
mother's wand. She turned her own
ears into bat wings and flew away, far across
the sea, to a land where the Boo-Hoo Witches
would never find her.

"The young girl buried that wicked wand in a meadow where nobody would find it," said Jill. "Then she went to start a new life. A neat and tidy and helpful life."

"Here it comes ... I just know it ..." whispered Megan.

"And," said Minister Jill, "that young girl was me."

"Told you!" said Megan.

"You were going to be a witch? A properly bad witch?" said King Edwin. "That's terrible! But also kind of awesome! But also terrible! Hang on, why didn't you snap the wand, or burn it, or something?"

"You can only destroy the wand of a Boo-Hoo Witch with tears of happiness," said Minister Jill. "But those are rare. You don't see them a lot. Try crying one right now. See? You can't do it, can you? Now, what else happened apart from the antlers? Please tell me you didn't cast any spells."

"Well, umm, well ..." said Megan, "there was an accident and ... we kind of made it shoot out magic lightning. Which lit up the whole sky."

Jill jumped to her feet, then grabbed the chair, panting. Then she hiccupped. The hiccup was nothing to do with being afraid. She'd just eaten some baguette too quickly.

"Was it bright enough that somebody – like a witch with a telescope – could see it from far across the sea?" said Jill.

"Don't worry, Jill," said Edwin. "I bet the Boo-Hoo Witches won't come to Edwinland.

Things will be fine because things normally are.
That's just how the world works!"

Then the sky outside turned as dark as
three midnights in a jug.

Nobody spoke. They all knew what it meant.

The Boo-Hoo Witches were already here.

Invasion of the Witches

"This is a slightly tricky moment," said Jill, who really meant 'this is a hugely massively dangerous moment' but didn't want to scare the others. "Megan, Edwin, stand behind me. Stay quiet and let me do the talking. Whatever you do, don't let them know I've got the wand behind my back."

Staying quiet would be hard for Edwin.
He was nine years old. Nine-year-olds
are made for doing noisy
stuff, like banging metal
trays on their heads and
eating crisps while
holding a megaphone.
But Edwin would
try his
very best.

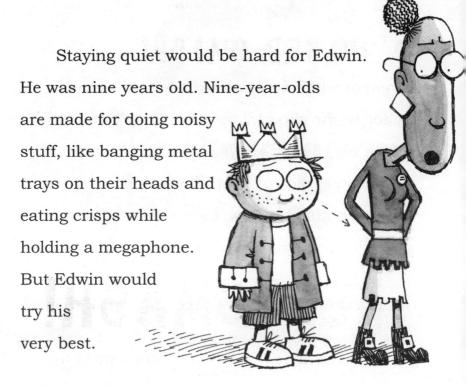

KER-SMASH!

A witch on a broomstick crashed through a
window.

NO KER-SMASH!

Another witch flew silently through the hole made in the glass by the first. That didn't feel like a big enough entrance. So she flew around to the other side of King Edwin's throne room, found another window, then rode her broom straight through it with an even bigger

KER-SMASH!

The terrifying Boo-Hoo Witches stood in the throne room. There are two main kinds of witches: tall beautiful ones, and shrivelled ones with warty noses. The Boo-Hoo Witches had one of each.

The tall beautiful one had wonderfully curly hair with clowngrumble highlights. Her long coat swished along the floor. It looked like it was made out of small cute creatures who probably never woke up one day and said, "Hey! We're tired of being cute AND alive, so please turn us into a fur coat!"

That witch really is beautiful, thought Edwin. *If I was a teenage king, I would probably fall in love with her and want to kiss her, and then, oh! One kiss from her ruby lips would turn me into an ice statue.*

But Edwin was only nine – too young to fall in love with her. Instead, he decided she just looked like a bit of a show-off.

The beautiful witch wrote a squiggle in the air with her wand, and a glowing name plate appeared over her head. She was called Zanzoo.

The shrivelled warty one had the classic witchy look: hunched back, huge hooked nose. But what made her special was that her nose had another smaller hooked nose on it. The nose had a nose. And her nose-nose had a tiny nose-nose-nose.

That must be very rare, thought Edwin. *If I ever make collectable cards of my enemies, she will be a valuable shiny one.*

The triple-nosed witch gave herself a magic glowing name plate too. She was called Grebb.

"Jill, you poor darling!" said Zanzoo. "You've been stranded in this sorry little kingdom all these years, have you? I'm so pleased we saw that magic lightning, or we never would have found you!"

"Cackle!" said Grebb.

"Jill, we're here to save you. You're coming home with us," said Zanzoo.

"I'm staying just where I am," said Minister Jill.

"And she's got nothing behind her back," said Megan. Then she clamped her hands over her mouth.

"Whoops. Again," said the jester, through her fingers.

Jill whipped out the wand, levelled it at
Zanzoo and uttered a spell.

WAND THAT I KEEP
IN A TIN,
THROW THESE
WITCHES IN THE—

But before Minister Jill
could say the word 'bin', Zanzoo

twiddled her own magic wand – and Jill's wand flew straight to the tall witch, who put it in her pocket.

"Cackle!" said Grebb.

"Excuse me, madam. Is 'cackle' the only word you can say?" said King Edwin. Even when evil witches had invaded his castle, he couldn't stop himself being polite. Edwin was such a nice boy.

"Cackle!" said Grebb, which more or less answered his question.

"Oh, I promised to shut up, didn't I?" said Edwin. "Don't mind me. Just carry on, everyone."

"Jill, have you been babysitting this silly little boy-king all this time?" said Zanzoo. "So sweet. And such a waste of your talents. Come along, Jill my poppet. Wand, hear my call, and make Jill small!"

That was a shrinking spell. In the time it takes to scratch your bum twice, Jill shrunk to the size of a finger and was sucked into Zanzoo's handbag.

"We'll make her a wicked Boo-Hoo Witch!" said Zanzoo. "And when there are three of us once more, we'll make the whole world cry forever! We shall be UNSTOPPABLE!"

Edwin had to save Jill. But how?

I've got a sword and a helmet, thought Edwin, *but they're upstairs in my cupboard under my box of comics. There's nothing here that I can fight the witches with. Wait, there's breakfast! Maybe I can fight them with breakfast!*

King Edwin stuck a cereal box on his head. Then he pushed a baguette through a piece of toast. It wasn't as good as his real sword and helmet, but it would have to do.

"Zanzoo, give me back my minister!" said Edwin. "And, oh yeah,

make her big again so a puppy doesn't eat
her by mistake." He swung his baguette-toast-
sword, but not too quickly in case it snapped
in half.

Grebb twiddled her wand and said, "Cackle
cackle!" The baguette-toast-sword turned into a
giant slimy slug.

"EURGH!" said Edwin, dropping the slug,
which oozed around in circles on the floor,
wondering who on earth it was and where
it had just come
from.

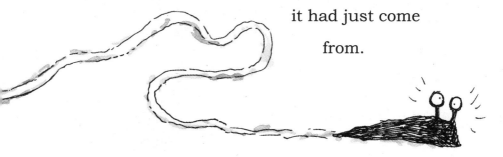

"She's ours now, you silly child!" said
Zanzoo, sweetly. "Feel free to cry as much
as you like. Crying just makes us stronger!
Hahahaha!"

"Cackle!" said Grebb.

Then the two witches jumped on their
brooms and ZOOMED out of the window.

And Jill was gone with them.

What to Do Now

Right, thought King Edwin Flashypants, *this is bad. I can't run the kingdom without Jill. The Boo-Hoo Witches stole her, and I never even told Jill how important she is to me, and it's too late now because they're going to make her just like them, all evil and stuff, and the Boo-Hoo Witches will rule the world and it's all my stupid fault for*

going in The Weird Meadow and I'm like totally
the worst king in the universe.

Then he realised just what he had to do next.

"Megan?" said Edwin. "Stand back, because
I'm going to have a bit of a panic."

Edwin ran around the throne room,
flapping his arms and screaming.

"AAAAAAAAAAAAAAAHHHH!" said Edwin.

He ran along every single corridor in the
castle.

"AAAAAAAAAAAAAAAAHHHHHHH!"

Then he ran all over the battlements, up and down the stairs, and around and around the seat of his king-size toilet.

King Edwin only stopped when he ran into the throne room again and Megan slapped him round the face with a cold fried egg left over from breakfast.

"You can't panic!" said Megan. "Well, you can for a little bit, because you're only nine. But you're also a king. And kings have to know what to do. I don't know what to do because I'm a jester and my job is being super-foolish."

"You're right, Megan," said Edwin as he wiped the yolk off his face with his sleeve. Something Jill would never let him do. "If I'm going to stop the Boo-Hoo Witches turning Jill into one of them, I can't let my loaf get freaked."

Edwin took a few seconds to un-freak his loaf, and then he felt a lot better.

Then he thought: *What would Jill do?*

"Let's make a list," said Edwin. So they did.

Edwin chewed his pencil until the little rubber came off the end. *Making lists isn't helping so much after all,* thought Edwin. *Also I should spit this rubber into the bin because it's*

not the tastiest one I've ever chewed, and I've chewed loads.

"There's one thing we have which they don't," said Megan.

"Ooh! What's that?" said the king.

At the bottom of the 'what we have' list, Megan wrote: 'Megan has a sore thumb'.

Yes, lists were definitely no use.

"Let's go to the library!" said King Edwin. "Books have facts – maybe even facts about these witches."

"Not sure I can come, Your Majesty," said Megan. "The antlers have disappeared, but I think I've just turned into a piano."

Edwin looked at Megan's keyboard. Then he looked at her lid and her pedals.

Yes, she's turned into a piano, thought Edwin.

The king was a very clever boy who was good at working things out quickly.

"There's something strange going on with you, Megan," said Edwin. "As soon as we've got Jill back, we must find out what."

"Good idea," said Megan.

Edwin loved the castle library, because it was full of amazing books, and because you could scoot around on the book trolley, at least until somebody told you off.

Since moving to Edwin's castle, Edwin's friend Baxter the Hermit had worked as the librarian. Baxter loved books so much he made a coat and a pet dog out of them.

"Sorry, I've looked on all the shelves, Your Majesty," said Baxter. "But I can't find any books about Boo-Hoo Witches. And nor can Mister Flappy Pages."

Baxter patted the book dog. One of its ears fell off.

"But let's see if I can find you something to help fight them, young man!" said Baxter.

He disappeared behind some tall shelves. Edwin heard a squeaky pen noise.

Baxter came out holding one of his flip-flops – but now it had 'ANTI-WITCH FLIP-FLOP' written on the bottom.

"It's an Anti-Witch Flip-Flop," said Baxter.

Edwin couldn't see how a flip-flop would be any use against Zanzoo and Grebb, but he tucked it in his coat anyway, just to be polite.

"Well, there's one thing we know," Edwin said to Megan, as he played 'Old McDonald Had a Farm' on her. "Jill said the witches live far away across the ocean on the Island of the Weeping Willow. If we get a boat and sail it far away, wherever 'far away' is exactly, we'll be sure to find them. And Jill, too."

Edwin found Jill's old rowing boat. It didn't look quite comfy enough for a long trip, so he built a living room on the top. Then he built a

bedroom on top
of that, then a
bathroom, then a
games room, then
a toy cupboard
right on the
very top.

"I wish Jill
was here," said
King Edwin
Flashypants. "She'd
tell us we're taking
way too much stuff,
and she'd be right."

"We could just tell each other that instead,"
said Megan, who wasn't a piano any more, but
had the head of an hippopotamus.

"We could, or we could load some more cool
stuff on the boat," said Edwin.

"More cool stuff!" said Megan. So they stacked the boat with dot-to-dot puzzle books, board games, a jar of ants for Megan to eat, footballs, and coloured string in case Edwin had an idea for a new kind of slide.

Everyone in Edwinland came to the beach to wave Edwin and Megan goodbye.

"Hope you find Minister Jill soon!" said one villager.

"Please don't die a horrible death!" said Baxter.

"We'll try not to!" said Edwin.

"If you do have to die a death, just make it a nice one!" said Baxter.

"Okey dokey!" said Edwin.

Megan pulled on the oars, saying, "Ouch! Ouch! Ouch! Don't worry, I'm fine. Ouch! Ouch!" because her thumb was still sore.

From across the ocean, over the sound of crashing waves, Edwin thought he could hear that strange sad voice once again – but a little louder this time. He could make out a few more of the words.

*Something-something so **much that I***
***Can't find** something-something it*
*So something-something-something **bloop***
***Wonkargle**-something-something.*

I'm sad too, thought Edwin. *Sad and scared for Jill. But I mustn't cry, I mustn't! Crying makes the magic of the Boo-Hoo Witches stronger!*

So, to stop himself from crying, he screwed up his face and whistled and pulled his hair and blew raspberries, which was all great fun for the seagulls to watch.

The Island of the Weeping Willow

Across the ocean, on the Island of the Weeping Willow, Zanzoo and Grebb walked round and round Minister Jill – who was full size again now.

Grebb was allergic to weeping willow trees. But weeping willows went well with the whole

'making people cry' thing that the Boo-Hoo
Witches loved, so the tree had to stay, even
though it made Grebb sneeze a lot.

"Cackle-choo! Cackle-choo!"

Three noses made her sneezes extra-powerful. She blasted herself a little way into the air each time.

"Such a shame about King Edwin," said Zanzoo. "He hasn't cried once since we took you away. If he had, I would have felt a teensy magic tingle."

Zanzoo made a sad pouty face.

"Maybe he doesn't love you so very much after all, Jill my little chestnut."

"He does love me," said Jill. "He doesn't always remember to say it, but ..."

"Oh, really?" Zanzoo smiled. "What does he say then?"

Jill remembered what Edwin said the day before he went to The Weird Meadow: "I just don't know why you're here."

Is that how Edwin really thinks about me? thought Jill. *It can't be, can it?*

"Oh, you don't know what to say about Edwin now, do you?" said Zanzoo. "But don't worry about that ungrateful little scamp another second, Jill dear! Grebb and I forgive you for running away. Why? Because we love you. That's why – finally – you're going to be one of us."

"Never!" said Jill. "I'll never be a Boo-Hoo Witch. That's why I ran away years ago."

Zanzoo put her hand on Minister Jill's ribs. And frowned.

"Ah, there's the problem," said Zanzoo. "You haven't got a witch's heart. Yours feels warm, like a normal human's. A true witch heart is cold, my dear, so very cold. But ... I think we can fix you."

"Cackle-**CHOO!**" said Grebb, sneezing just high enough for her pointy hat to get stuck in a branch of the tree.

Meanwhile, King Edwin and Megan the Jester voyaged far across the southern seas in their rowing boat. They journeyed for hours, and days, and a bit of a week, and a couple of minutes and then some more hours and a few ticks and a bagful of tocks. Time gets jumbled up when you're out at sea because the waves toss it around so much.

They found all sorts of strange and wonderful islands.

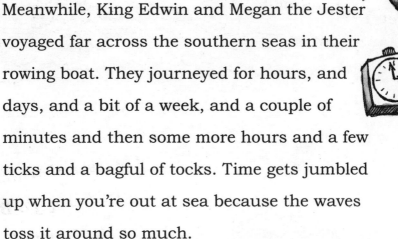

(THEY MAKE GOOD SUNSHADES)

The Island Of The Giant Foot Guys

The Island Where All The Farts Go After You've Smelt Them

The Island Which Turned Out To Be A Sea Monster's Head

The Island Which Is The Exact Size And Shape Of A Hairy Finger

The Island of Rabbits Who Say "Machunga Machunga"

The Island of the Upside Down Ballerinas

The Island of Spare Islands

But wherever they went, they couldn't find
The Island of the Weeping Willow.

"We can't find the Island of the Weeping
Willow," said Edwin as he chewed on his fifth
toffee of the afternoon. "What if we don't get to
Jill before they make her a Boo-Hoo Witch? And
I wish she was here to remind me to eat healthy
snacks. Like those apples, those ones there, in
that bowl that's right in front of me."

"Oh dear, I'm frowning," Megan said,
frowning. She now had her normal head again,
but with big elephant ears.

"Megan? Would you like me to let off an
air horn right in your face?" said Edwin. "That
normally cheers you up."

"Sorry, Your Majesty," said Megan.

"I don't think that even an air horn right in the face would work on me today. I'm so afraid for Minister Jill."

Just then they heard some loud and jolly singing outside the window. They ran downstairs and outside to see where it was coming from.

A shoal of mermen and mermaids were dancing and diving on the crest of a wave. Real live merpeople. Half human, half fish. Edwin thought people just drew them around the edge of maps to make the maps look cool, but here they were for reals.

And the singing! It was like no singing Edwin had ever heard. It was full of joy in just the way that the strange sad singing wasn't. And the song the merpeople sang seemed to be called 'We Are the Best At Singing'. Every line of it said

'We are the best at singing'.

"Greetings, merpeople!" said Edwin. "I am King Edwin Flashypants of Edwinland. I'm looking for my friend Jill who was taken by the Boo-Hoo Witches, to the Island of the Weeping Willow."

The merpeople all looked at each other and smiled.

"Island, you say!" said one merman. "Oh, my boy, we are the folk of the sea. We know where all the islands are!"

"We are not just the best at singing, we are the best at leading the way!" said a mermaid. "Come, young king and your faithful elephant! You'll soon see your witches!"

Finally, a bit of luck, thought Edwin. *If Jill was here, she wouldn't mind me having another toffee to celebrate. And then another seven toffees, because you know, toffees.*

Edwin emptied the rest of the pack into his mouth. So he didn't notice the fish fin that followed their boat.

Cutting through the waves.

Never slowing.

The Thing About Mermaids

Edwin and Megan's boat bounced over the surging ocean. For extra speed, Megan opened her elephant ears to the wind like billowing sails.

"Nearly there!" said a smiling merman as he plucked his eyebrows in a little mirror. He had

the broadest chest you ever saw, and below it
not a six-pack but a fifteen-pack. He carried a
trident. That's a spear with three points – just
the kind of spear that's handy for catching fish.

Edwin wondered if
merpeople really did eat fish.
If they did, he thought, would
that make them cannibals?
Or would it not count if it
was the human end of the
mermaid doing the eating? If a
mermaid is hungry, are they allowed
to eat their own tail? And if they ate
all of themselves would they just
vanish? Or turn inside out? Or
would they eat themselves
into another dimension that
smells of chips and vinegar?

I only just found out where all the farts go, thought Edwin. *But as soon as I answer one question, another five pop up from nowhere. Why? Oh. That's another question. Should I keep a list of all the questions? Ah! That was another!*

Finally the boat slid on to a sandy beach. King Edwin looked around for a weeping willow tree.

He couldn't see one. But he could see, not far away, a castle.

And a slide. With two loop-the-loops.

They were back on the shore of Edwinland.

"Here you are!" chuckled a mermaid. "This beach, WHICH IS the one you started from.

Get it? Which ... is. Witches! Which ... is! Sounds like 'witches'!"

"We're not just the best at singing! We are the best at being funny! Ha ha ha!" said the broad-chested merman, stopping for a moment to shave around his belly button.

Edwin and Megan had been led all the way back home – just for a silly joke.

The king was trying very very hard not to cry. He didn't want to give the Boo-Hoo Witches one drop of magic power. He tried pulling his hair and blowing raspberries again, but this time it didn't work. Big fat angry tears sprayed out of his face and splooshed on the sand.

"Well, I don't think it's funny!" said Edwin. "Our friend Jill is in terrible danger from the Boo-Hoo Witches, and we've got to find her or horrible things will happen, and now we're further from her than ever, you scaly bumboils!"

"You should all be ashamed of yourselves, tricking a child," said Megan. She'd just grown an elephant's trunk to go with the ears, so she threw in some furious trumpeting.

"Yes, we've been thoughtless and cruel," said the biggest merman, bowing his beautifully bearded head.

"We're sorry, Your Majesty," said the prettiest mermaid as she combed her long, long hair.

"Ha ha! Not really!" said a cute little mermaid. "We had you again! We aren't just the best at being funny – we're the best at being funny twice! What a stupid little boy-king you are!"

Booming with laughter, the merpeople flipped back into the waves and wriggled out to sea.

I haven't finished telling them off yet! Edwin thought. *And when I've finished telling them off they're going to stay told off!*

Edwin grabbed the oars and rowed after the merpeople.

Grrrrrrr, thought Edwin.

"He's even stupider than Sally!" said the cute little mermaid.

And who is Sally? And also grrrrrrr again, thought Edwin.

And all the time, the fish fin followed the boat.

Cutting through the waves.

Never slowing.

On Weeping Willow Island, Zanzoo and Grebb
shivered and smiled and their skin crackled
with magic energy.

"Mmmmm, delicious!" said
Zanzoo."I just felt
your silly ickle
king cry.

But I really don't think it's because he misses you, Jill my dear. I think it's because there's nobody to bring him sweeties."

"I suppose you're right," said Jill, but really Jill was thinking: *I bet Edwin is thinking of me. If only I could find him. If I can just reach my old wand I could use it to fly away again ...*

Minister Jill's hand slowly reached for Zanzoo's pocket.

"Oovey boovey, you no-movey!" said Zanzoo, and suddenly Jill was frozen to the spot. The only thing the minister could move was her head.

"Caught you, you cheating little minx!" said Zanzoo. "Oh, you'll get your wand back soon enough, my dear. After we've cast a Heart Chiller spell. Then you'll be as wicked as we are! Grebb, on a scale of one to five, how wicked will Jill become?"

Grebb held up seven fingers.

"Grebb, bring the magic potion!" said Zanzoo.

"Cackle-choo!" said Grebb, hauling a big steaming cauldron out from the hole in the tree

where the Boo-Hoo Witches lived.

"It's made with juice from the rotten eyeballs of murdered toads," said Zanzoo. "And vulture guts from vultures who only eat snail sick, and just a dash of minotaur wee. No potion is stronger! Grebb and I will take a sip each, then our wicked magic will double in power! Ha ha!"

Zanzoo held a cup of the stuff next to her lips. She smelled it. She was totally definitely going to drink it.

A bee flew past, sniffed the potion once, died, and fell into the cup.

"But, thinking about it," said Zanzoo, putting the cup down, "we've probably got enough magic power for this spell already."

Zanzoo and Grebb pointed their own wands at Jill. Zanzoo chanted.

"There's something very wrong with Jill—
Of humans she's too fond!
But our spell will make her cruel—
Then she'll take her mother's—"

Just as Zanzoo was about to say 'wand', she looked down at the wand sticking out of her pocket.

"JILL! WHAT HAVE WE ALWAYS SAID ABOUT LOOKING AFTER YOUR WAND?" bellowed Zanzoo. "THERE'S A BIT OF YOURS MISSING!"

Minister Jill looked. Yes – the tip of the wand was all splintery.

"You may NOT be a Boo-Hoo Witch with a broken wand!" said Zanzoo. "We must find the splinter! FIND THE SPLINTER!"

And Zanzoo and Grebb zoomed away on their brooms.

Jill was left all alone on the island, apart from a few birds who looked down at her from the weeping willow tree.

"Hello, birds," said Jill. "They put a spell on me so I can't move, and I'm right under you, so please nobody do a poo on my shoe."

SPLOOT

8.

Sally

Edwin rowed and rowed, and growled and growled. He was still furious with the merpeople, even though he'd been rowing for a whole hour and he couldn't even see them any more.

"You swimmy horrors!" shouted Edwin.

"I think they've gone underwater," said Megan.

Edwin didn't think they could hear him underwater, so he wrote 'you swimmy horrors' on a wooden plank, then threw it in the sea upside down so the merpeople could read it if they ever looked up.

The wind began to howl. It blew Edwin's crown off. Luckily he caught it with his foot before it plopped into the ocean.

"Umm, Your Majesty," said Megan, "I think you were so angry you rowed us into a big storm without noticing. Also, your foot is wearing the crown now, so is your foot the new king? King Foot the First?"

Edwin jammed the crown back on his head and looked at the sea. A big wave rolled towards them.

"It's okay," said Edwin as it splashed over the boat. "It was just a big wave, not a giant huge wave."

He looked up and saw a giant huge wave heading for them.

"Not so bad," he said as that wave crashed

on to the boat and flooded the bottom room.

"Sure, that was a giant huge wave, but not a

colossal vast mega-wave."

"Umm, Your Majesty—" said Megan the Jester, pointing with her trunk at the colossal vast mega-wave coming right at them.

The colossal vast mega-wave picked their small boat up like it was a small boat – and **SMASHED** it down again. The boat fell to bits, even though Edwin had lashed it together with every colour of string that he had.

King Edwin and Megan the Jester clung on to the 'you swimmy horrors' plank. There they were, helpless in a raging sea.

"Maybe I'll change into something that floats! That would be so useful!" said Megan.

Megan changed into a brick.

"Sorry!" said Megan.

We'll never find Jill in time now, thought Edwin as he held brick-Megan above the water.

"Try not to think about that fish fin heading right for us, which probably belongs to a shark, let's face it," said Megan. "Things are bad enough without worrying about that too. Just don't think about how it cuts through the waves, never slowing."

A fish face popped out of the water.

said the face.

So they did.

Half an hour later the storm had blown away –
storms are always doing that – and King Edwin
Flashypants and Megan the Jester sat on a little
sandy island, wrapped in towels, drinking hot
chocolate and trying
to warm up.

"I'm Sally," said Sally. "And I think you're wondering just what I am."

She was right, they were. Sally had the bottom half of a human being, but the top half of a fish.

"I'm a reverse mermaid," said Sally. "I'm a different way round from the others and that's why they're mean to me. I had the feeling they'd pull some nasty prank on you, so I've been following you for a while."

"Well, if I was giving out awards for not-niceness, they'd get a big trophy with lions for handles," said Megan, who wasn't the size and shape of a brick any more, but had a baked potato for a nose.

"I was born a normal mermaid but when I was a baby some witches came along and swapped me round," said Sally. "It's hard. I cry a lot."

"It was the Boo-Hoo Witches, I'll bet!" said Edwin.

"The other merpeople are so horrible to me that I have to live away from them on this island," said Sally. "And mermaids are supposed

to comb their hair! But I don't have any. And all
mermaids sing, but my song always comes out
so sad. It's a song about love and I've got no one
to sing it to."

And Sally sang – with that
same sweet, sad voice that Edwin
had heard from far across the sea.

I love you so much that I
Can't find the words to say it
So I'll make some up: ger-blinji-bloop
Wonkargle-mamzi-blay-it.

And though my words sound sort of strange
Each one is made with love
So here's some more: gwuh-skarpy-parp
Ger-wimbly, wombly, wuvvvv.

The reverse mermaid's tale made them all
feel pretty miserable. Megan tried to sniff, but
her baked potato just waggled up and down.

Sally looked at the potato, then at Megan's

sore thumb. A fish doesn't exactly have a chin, but she stroked her fin roughly where her chin would be if it did.

"Megan, do you always have a baked potato for a nose?" said Sally.

"Not normally, no," said Megan.

"Then I think I know what your problem is," said Sally.

A few minutes later, Sally dug into Megan's thumb with some tweezers, and pulled out a little chunk of wood. Straight away, Megan's nose was just a nose.

Megan checked her arms. Two! She checked her head. No antlers! She checked her

body. She was fairly sure it wasn't a piano, or a
brick, or a laundry basket, or a gas barbecue,
or a packet of wine gums, or any of the other
things it had been lately. Megan was very
Megan-shaped.

"I'M CURED!"
said Megan, giving
Sally a big hug.

"OW!" said Sally, because one of Megan's jangly jester bells had got caught in her gills.

"So it was just a splinter all along!" said Edwin.

Sally looked at the little sharp thing. "Looks like it. Making her thumb sore AND making her body do peculiar things."

"It's a piece of Jill's wand! From when Megan grabbed it in the meadow!" said Edwin.

And then Edwin's mind began to fizz like a bottle of cream soda that you open just after it's been bouncing around in a shopping bag. He just knew he was having a really big idea.

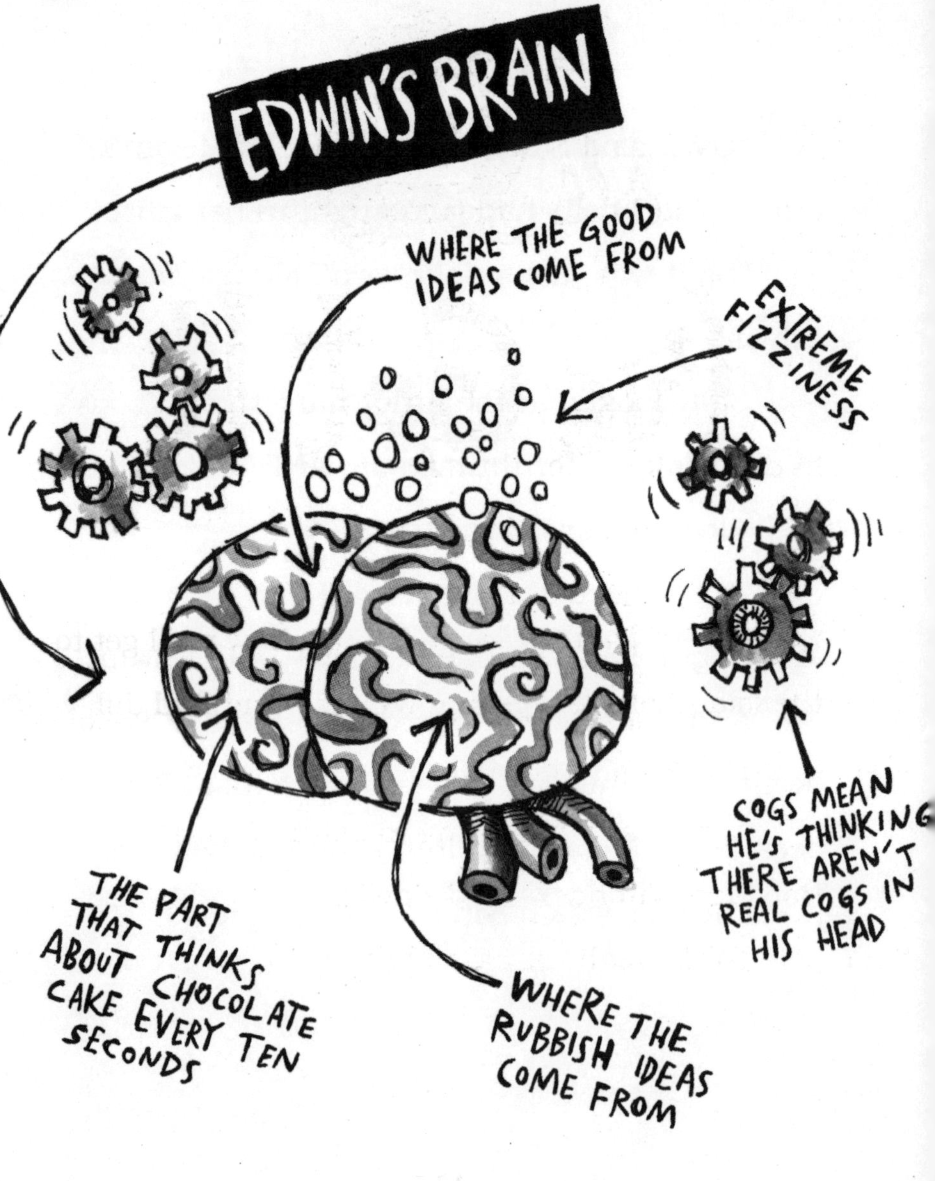

EDWIN'S BRAIN

WHERE THE GOOD IDEAS COME FROM

EXTREME FIZZINESS

THE PART THAT THINKS ABOUT CHOCOLATE CAKE EVERY TEN SECONDS

WHERE THE RUBBISH IDEAS COME FROM

COGS MEAN HE'S THINKING THERE AREN'T REAL COGS IN HIS HEAD

I've Got It

"I've got it!" said the king. "I know how we'll get to the Island of the Weeping Willow – and find Jill."

"I'll help," said Sally.

"Because we're going to get back at the Boo-Hoo Witches?" said Edwin.

"Well, yeah, but also because you're a boy

and a jester who rowed a rubbish boat right into a storm and I'm a bit worried about you both."

Edwin held up the splinter and said, "We'll keep this piece of wand safe in a jam jar. Then we'll say a rhyme asking it to point the way to Weeping Willow Island. Then all we need to do is build a new raft and keep sailing to wherever it points!"

"Genius!" said Megan. "Oh, Sally, you wouldn't believe the trouble that wand has brought with it. Ha ha! Guess what I did on the night we found it?"

"Don't actually say the words, though, Megan," said Edwin.

"This sign told us not to make a rhyme near the wand in case it cast a spell," said Megan. "So guess what I went and said! Ha ha ha! I am such a dummy!"

"But don't use the words Megan ..." said Edwin. But there was no stopping Megan now.

"I said, 'Imagine if it shot out lightning. Wouldn't that be awfully frightening!'"

And a second later, the splinter was shooting huge crackling bolts in orange, purple, green and clowngrumble all over the place. The sky lit up.

"I didn't think it would do it again," said Megan.

"I did," said Edwin.

"You could have warned me," said Megan.

The Boo-Hoo Witches had flown to Edwin's castle, where they were rampaging around

looking for the missing splinter. They threw
over Edwin's throne, ripped up his best velvet
cushions, and kicked Mr
Flappy Pages to bits. Anyone
who tried to stop them got
zapped until
their hair
smoked.

"Tiny little splinter of wood, come to me just like you should!" said Zanzoo, thrashing her wand in the air.

But the tiny piece of wand couldn't be found anywhere.

Grebb burst into the throne room.

"Cackle!" said Grebb.

"Grebb, my dear, sometimes I just don't know what 'cackle' means."

"Cackle! Cackle cackle! Cackle cackle cackle cackle cackle cackle!" said Grebb, windmilling her stubby arms.

"No, still no idea," said Zanzoo.

Grebb grabbed Zanzoo's coat, pulled her outside, and pointed her wartiest finger out to sea. Far away, flashes of green, blue and clowngrumble danced through the clouds.

"That's where the splinter is!" said Zanzoo. "Follow that magic lightning!"

The witches jumped on their brooms and *SWOONNSHHH!* Off they sped.

On Sally's island, Edwin was lying down with his feet in the air.

I need to have another great idea but my brain's still exhausted from having the last great idea, he thought, *so if I lie like this, my blood will pour down into my brain and make me clever.*

"The Boo-Hoo Witches might already be flying here really fast to get the little splinter of wand," said Edwin. "They love wands. That's a thing we know. And when they get it they will fly away and ... Aha!"

Edwin sat up.

"I know how we find Jill! The witches will take us to her. All we need is a plank of wood and some very long string."

Wood was easy – they still had the plank with 'you swimmy horrors' written on it. String was harder. Sally didn't have any on her island, and all of Edwin's string had gone down with the boat.

"Don't suppose the next island along is called The Island With all the String Shops?" said Megan.

Sally shook her head.

Edwin got the magic splinter from the jam jar they'd caught it in.

"Pianos have strings," said Edwin. "Megan, this is going to sound weird, but put this magic splinter back in your thumb for a minute. You've been a piano before. You just need to think very piano-ey thoughts and see if you can become a piano again."

"I'll try," said Megan, and she jabbed her thumb with the splinter.

Then Megan thought piano thoughts. *Piano piano piano piano piano,* thought Megan. *Piano piano piano, I am SUCH a piano. Piano piano*

piano piano piano, great big piano-ey piano. Piano

piano piano piano piano piano piano piano piano

who's-a-lovely-piano-then. Piano, piano.

And there she was – a piano.

"Quick," said Edwin, "open her lid and get a

few piano strings!"

That's just what Edwin and Sally did. Then Edwin pulled the splinter out again, and Megan was a normal jester once more.

"Just a couple more things to do, then we'll be ready," said Edwin.

Fifteen minutes later, the sky turned as dark as five-and-a-quarter midnights in a jug, and the Boo-Hoo Witches WHOOSHED on to Sally's island. The words 'here is the magic splinter' were written in big letters on the sand, and next to them was the splinter in the jam jar.

"Cackle!" said Grebb, as she rushed to the jar and tipped out the tiny piece of wood.

"That was easy. Surprisingly easy," said

Zanzoo. "Good! Now, back to the weeping willow!

Jill will be a Boo-Hoo Witch by nightfall!"

The witches hopped back on their brooms and hurtled across the sea.

The Boo-Hoo Witches hadn't noticed a nine-year-old boy sneak out from the bushes, and tie a piece of piano string around Grebb's broom when she was getting the splinter.

And they didn't notice a jester hanging onto
the string, waterskiing across the ocean with a
boy and a fish-girl sitting on her shoulders.

Edwin, Megan and Sally were coming to
save Jill.

Fruit

When the witches got back to their island, Grebb stuck six corks up her various nostrils to stop the big weeping willow from making her sneeze.

"Cackle!" said Grebb.

Jill was still frozen with the no-movey spell, so all she could do was watch in horror while Zanzoo glued the tiny splinter back into Jill's wand.

"And now your wand is complete, Jill my little wafer biscuit!" said Zanzoo. "All ready for you, right after we've transformed you into the wickedest Boo-Hoo Witch of all! You won't care about stupid little Edwin then!"

Then Zanzoo came very close to Jill and whispered in her ear.

"You don't know what it's like, Jill! It's just me and Grebb in the Boo-Hoo Witches, and she only ever says one word! Just one! I'm dying for some real conversation."

"See?" whispered Zanzoo. "I can't take it

any more! I need you here!"

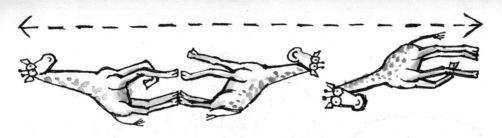

Imagine a giraffe lying down. Imagine another giraffe lying down near it, just for fun. Imagine a third giraffe lying down because it thinks that's just what giraffes have to do nowadays. So they're all making a line now, a line exactly three giraffes long. That's how far away Edwin, Sally and Megan were as they spied on the witches from behind a rock. It would have been easier to say 'about fifteen metres' but it's too late now. Oh well.

"There's Jill!" Megan gasped. "And they're about to change her forever! But it's fine because Edwin must have a plan for this part, too."

Sally and Megan looked at Edwin.

Edwin looked at the sky, then his
fingernails, then the tip of his nose. Anything so
long as he didn't have to look them in the eye.

"I was thinking so hard about how to get to the island," said Edwin, "so I suppose didn't think so much about how to beat the witches when we got here. I thought 'Later Me' would work that out, but now it is later and I am Later Me. It's funny how that keeps happening."

It's hard to tell when a fish face doesn't look impressed. But Edwin looked at Sally and thought, *That fish face doesn't look impressed.*

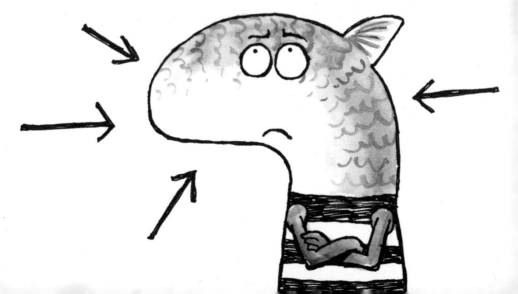

"So," said Sally, "you brought us to the Island of the Weeping Willow, but somehow you forgot to—"

"The willow!" said Edwin. "It really is quite twisty. The branches turn this way and that and even do loop-the-loops. It's just like my slide back home! And I'm very good at sliding."

"It's true, he is. I've got pictures," said Megan the Jester.

Edwin said, "I'll slide down a branch, maybe that one there, then I'll fly through the air and knock the Boo-Hoo Witches right over! Then I'll grab Jill and we'll run away."

"But what about the witches' magic

powers?" said Sally. "Plus we're on an island, so we can't run far. There's that too."

"Oh, I'll have a great idea about that once I'm hurtling through the air," said Edwin. "I have some of my best ideas while I'm hurtling."

Edwin climbed up the dangly bits of the willow, then slid down a branch.

WHOOSH! Around the first loop –

ZIP! Around the second loop –

Meanwhile, Zanzoo and Grebb pointed their wands at Jill, ready to cast the Heart-Chiller spell.

"There's something very wrong with Jill," chanted Zanzoo. "Of humans she's too—DUCK!"

The witches ducked. King Edwin Flashypants whooshed over their heads and thumped into the ground.

"Edwin! You came for me!" said Jill.

"How DARE you interrupt my spell, boy?" said Zanzoo. "See that chap? Wand, go zap!"

And she shot stinging energy bolts at Edwin's head and bum.

"Nobody zaps that chap!" said Megan, running forward with Sally.

"Oh, bless, it's Edwin's big lump of a jester, come to save the day," said Zanzoo. "And what's this? Could it be that fish-girl we changed all those years ago? Deary me, what to do with you all?"

"Cackle cackle, cackle cackle!" said Grebb, flailing the air with her stubby wand.

In the blink of an eye, Edwin, Sally and Megan were transformed. They had become three pieces of fruit, hanging from the branches of the weeping willow.

"Oh, that's perfect, Grebb, you charming goblin!" said Zanzoo. "You three will dangle there forever on your stalks – and watch your precious Jill become as cruel and mean as we

are. I don't normally cackle. It's a habit for ugly witches, not beautiful ones like me. But just this once, I think I will."

And Zanzoo and Grebb cackled like, well, a pair of horrible witches.

The Heart

Edwin tried to move his arms.

He didn't have any.

He tried to move his legs.

He didn't have any.

He tried move his eyes.

Yes, he still had two of those, and the rest

of his face too. But being just a face on a piece of fruit isn't much use, when the person who's the nearest thing you've got to a mum is about to be turned into a dastardly witch by a heart-chilling magic spell.

It's all my fault, thought Edwin. *I went in The Weird Meadow, I did just what the signs said to not do. Jill's always done so much for me and I hardly noticed, and now she'll be a Boo-Hoo Witch, and we're just fruit, and I bet I'm not even a nice fruit but a horrible hairy fruit, one that tastes yucky.*

Edwin cried fruit juice tears.

"Yes, cry all you like, Edwin dear!" said Zanzoo. "Make us stronger!"

Once again the Boo-Hoo Witches levelled their wands at Jill.

"Right. THIS time!" said Zanzoo.

"There's something very wrong with Jill—
Of humans she's too fond.
But our spell will make her cruel—
Then she'll take her mother's wand!"

Streams of glowing magic power crackled from the witch's wands and hit Jill in the chest.

"OOOWWWW!" said Jill, because

apparently being turned evil stings a bit.

Edwin thought, *I still have a mouth. Maybe, before she turns all wicked and she isn't really Jill any more, I can tell her how much I love her.*

So Edwin sang the best song of love that he knew. He sang Sally's song, just for Jill.

"I love you so much that I
Can't find the words to say it
So I'll make some up: ger-blinji-bloop
Wonkargle-mamzi-blay-it ..."

The Boo-Hoo Witches' evil magic began to work on Jill. Wriggling into her heart. Trying to make it cruel and cold.

But something was pushing back.

Jill heard Edwin's song of love – and love is even more powerful than magic. In big enough amounts, anyway.

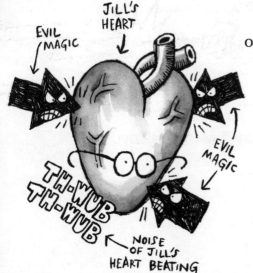

JILL'S HEART

EVIL MAGIC

EVIL MAGIC

TH·WUB TH·WUB TH·WUB

NOISE OF JILL'S HEART BEATING

"Her heart! It isn't chilling!" said Zanzoo.

"Grebb? Maximum power!"

"Cackle!" said Grebb.

With her other hand, Zanzoo pulled Jill's wand from her pocket. Now all three wands of the Boo-Hoo Witches blasted Jill with evil magic.

Sally and Megan joined in the singing.

And though my words sound sort of strange

Each one is made with love

So here's some more: gwuh-skarpy-parp

Ger-wimbly, wombly, wuvvvv ...

Jill was crying now. Not tears of sadness and fear which made the Boo-Hoo Witches stronger – no, she was crying tears of happiness, because she knew, she really knew at last, just how much Edwin loved her.

Edwin remembered something Jill said back in the castle.

Something about the only way to destroy the wand of a Boo-Hoo Witch ...

"Jill!" shouted King Edwin the Fruit. "Quick! There are tears of happiness! Running down your nose!"

Jill could only move her head – but that was enough. She puffed and puffed with her mouth and blew the tears off the tip of her nose.

The tears sprayed into the air – and on to the wands of the Boo-Hoo Witches.

With little FLUMFFS of clowngrumble-
coloured flame, all three wicked wands vanished
forever – and all the spells they ever cast winked
away.

"I can move again!" said Jill, wiggling her

arms. "And I'm pretty sure I've not been turned evil either. Look – a snail! Will I squash it?"

She waited a second.

"No I won't! There we are then. Definitely not evil."

CLUMP! BUMP! BLUMP! Edwin, Megan and Sally stopped being fruit, and fell down from the tree.

"CACKLLLE!" howled Grebb.

"MY WAAAAND!" wailed Zanzoo. "MY POWWWWERS! ALL GOOOOONE!"

"Yes, you'll never zap anyone again!" said Megan. "Also let me say 'oof', because it hurt when I fell, but I thought I'd say the other bit first."

"Even if we've lost our powers, we're as wicked as we ever were!" said Zanzoo. "And Jill's our prisoner!"

Zanzoo and Grebb seized Jill.

"Quickly, Grebb, to the getaway boat!" the beautiful witch said.

"Oh, nearly forgot!" said Edwin. "Baxter gave me this." Edwin pulled the Anti-Witch Flip-Flop from his coat and handed it to Megan. Edwin would have liked to be the big hero at

this moment, but he knew Megan had
the strongest arm, and the very best heroes –
like Edwin – know that even they need a bit of
hero help.

Megan hurled the flip-flop.

SLAP! went the flip-flop, right in Grebb's
face. It knocked all six corks out
of her nose.

"CA - CA - CA -" said Grebb, trying to find the corks on the ground. She was about to do an absolutely HUGE sneeze.

"CACKLE-

CHOO OOOO OO!!!"

Grebb shot into the air.

Zanzoo grabbed Grebb to stop her flying off the island – but the sneeze was so powerful that Grebb just took Zanzoo with her. They both tumbled into the sky.

Where did they land?

Edwin didn't care.

Megan didn't care.

Sally didn't either.

And maybe the person who didn't care the most was Jill. She'd been afraid of the Boo-Hoo Witches for her whole life. But she never would be again.

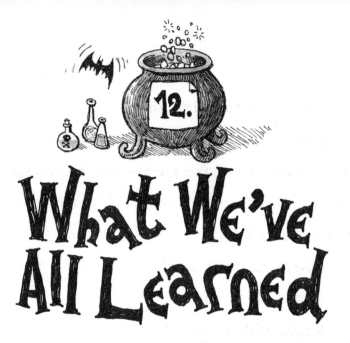

What We've All Learned

It took a while for Jill, Edwin and Megan to get

back to Edwinland. They had

to use a willow branch

as a raft and make a

sail out of all their

underwear.

Along the way, they stopped to tell the
mermaids and mermen that somebody was
giving out free ice-cream on 'that island over
there'. It was the Island of Giant Snarling Bears
Which Hate Merpeople, but for some reason
nobody remembered to tell the merpeople that.

Sometimes it's wrong to play tricks on people just because they played a trick on you. But sometimes it's absolutely fine.

Once the travellers were safely home, everyone in Edwinland gathered on the village green to hear what people had learned. This happened every time Edwin had an adventure. It helped everyone become a better person, and it was a good excuse for a cake sale.

Megan stood up first.

"I've learned something!" she said. "I've learned that if there's something wrong with you, like your thumb is sore, or you're growing antlers, or you're suddenly a piano, you should talk to someone who can help you. A doctor. Or a grown-up. Or a very clever fish-girl-thing."

Sally stood up.

"I've learned something," said Sally. "I've learned not to be sad about being a reverse mermaid. I met you lot, and you don't care which way round I am. I think that's why I didn't change back after the witches' wands went fwoomff."

"Great!" said Edwin. So you're a reverse mermaid – and you're going to own it?"

"I like the sound of that, Edwin," she said.

So Sally was the first person in the history of the world ever to 'own it'.

Then Jill stood up.

"I've learned something," said Jill. "I kept my witchy past a secret because I was ashamed. I thought you might all throw me out of Edwinland if you knew."

"We never would!" said everybody at exactly the same time.

"So from now on, I'll keep fewer secrets."

And she meant it, too. But Jill was still careful to say 'fewer secrets', not 'no secrets'.

"I've learned something," said Baxter. "I've learned that lobsters wee out of their faces."

Baxter didn't understand that you had to say things you learned on the adventure, not things you learned from a library book called *100 Amazing Animal Facts*. But nobody really minded.

Then Edwin stood up.

"I've learned two things," said Edwin. Everybody leaned forward. It was always a special treat when somebody had learned two things.

"Jill, I've learned that when you ask us not to do things, you're not trying to annoy us. It's normally because you love us and you want to keep us safe.

"But mostly – I've learned how important you are to me, Jill. I don't think I always let you know. But, from now on, I'll make sure I do."

With all the learning done, it was time
for a party. Megan played a new hit song
she'd written called 'You Be Freakin' My Loaf'.
Everybody sang, everybody danced, everybody
ate cake. They sang about dancing, they danced
about cake, they caked about singing.

Just before the sun went down, a shadow passed over the castle. The shadow of the huge icy mountain which towered above his kingdom. Hetherang-Dundister-Underploshy-Smeltus, it was called.

Edwin thought, *Maybe there* **is** *still a place in my kingdom I haven't been to ... The top of that mountain.*

Nobody had ever been all the way up. It was the tallest, iciest mountain for a thousand miles.

How would Edwin climb where nobody had ever climbed?

What would he discover when he was up there?

What was the secret of Hetherang-
Dundister-Underploshy-Smeltus?

We will find out.

In another book.

The End

CREDITS

Written and Drawn by
ANDY RILEY

Editor
EMMA GOLDHAWK

Designer
SAMUEL PERRETT

Publishing Director
ANNE MCNEIL

Mr Riley represented by
GORDON WISE

ALL RIGHT THEN...
What's Emperor Nurbison Doing?

EMPEROR NURBISON IS EDWIN'S ENEMY AND HE LIVES IN A SCARY CASTLE IN THE NEXT COUNTRY ALONG. BUT HOW'S HE BEEN FILLING HIS TIME WHILE KING EDWIN HAS THE ADVENTURE WITH THE BOO-HOO WITCHES?

LEARNING THE BANJO

PLUNG PLUNG PLUNG

EATING UNCOOKED SPAGHETTI TO SEE IF IT'S NICE

(IT'S NOT)

CUTTING TOENAILS

TALKING THROUGH A CROWN BECAUSE IT MAKES YOUR VOICE BIG AND ECHOEY

HOLDING BREATH FOR 60 SECONDS

STANDING VERY FAR AWAY

PAINTING A MODEL HORSE

KUNG FU

SLEEPING WHILE STANDING UP

DRINKING MILK

TOASTING MARSHMALLOWS
ON A CROWN

(BLOW
TORCH
TIED
TO A
STICK)

TRYING ON
A BEAR ONESIE

WHY AREN'T
I MOVING

MAKE
ME MOVE

TRYING TO GO
SLEDGING AFTER THE
SNOW STARTS MELTING

PRETENDING TO BE
A SEAGULL

BUT MOSTLY:

THINKING of HOW TO
DEFEAT KING EDWIN
FLASHYPANTS

ANDY RILEY has done lots of funny writing for film and TV, and he's even won prizes for it, like BAFTAs and an Emmy. He co-wrote the scripts for David Walliams's *Gangsta Granny* and *The Boy In The Dress*. Films he's written for include *Gnomeo & Juliet* and *The Pirates! In An Adventure With Scientists*. He wears cowboy hats a lot, and he's finally going to build a coracle this year, absolutely definitely.

 **www.facebook.com/KingFlashypants**